I KNOW WHERE THE FREIGHTERS GO

To Aunt Lucille
with love
Marti

WRITTEN & ILLUSTRATED BY
MARLENE MILLER

Ferne Press

I Know Where the Freighters Go
Copyright © 2008 by Marlene Miller
Printed in Canada

Summary: Do you remember the first time that you saw a freighter out on the Great Lakes? Did you try to imagine where it was headed and what it had onboard? This feeling of awe and wonder is captured in *I Know Where the Freighters Go*. From cargo to destination, and from the crew's jobs to buying groceries, all of our questions are answered in this engaging, lyrical, and delightfully illustrated story.

Library of Congress Cataloging-in-Publication Data
Miller, Marlene
I Know Where the Freighters Go/ Marlene Miller – First Edition
ISBN- 978-193391629-3
1. Freighters 2. Great Lakes 3. Maritime 4. Travel 5. Waterways 6. Cargo
I. Miller, Marlene II. Title. I Know Where the Freighters Go
Library of Congress Control Number: 2008931454

FERNE PRESS

Ferne Press is an imprint of Nelson Publishing & Marketing
366 Welch Road, Northville, MI 48167
www.nelsonpublishingandmarketing.com
(248) 735-0418

Dedication

To my parents, Norman and Peggy,
and to Jordan, Jacob, Jason, Kayla, and Jenna.

Acknowledgments

Thank you to my family and children for their love and support, to the volunteers at the Great Lakes Maritime Center at Vantage Point in Port Huron and at Boatnerd.com, to the U.S. Coast Guard, and to my sailing friends: Bob, Dave, Mark, and Sandy.

Special thanks to Diana Decker, a teacher whose five-day trip aboard the Paul R. Tregurtha, the Great Lakes' longest freighter at 1013 feet 6 inches, inspired this book. Diana provided details and photographs for the illustrations.

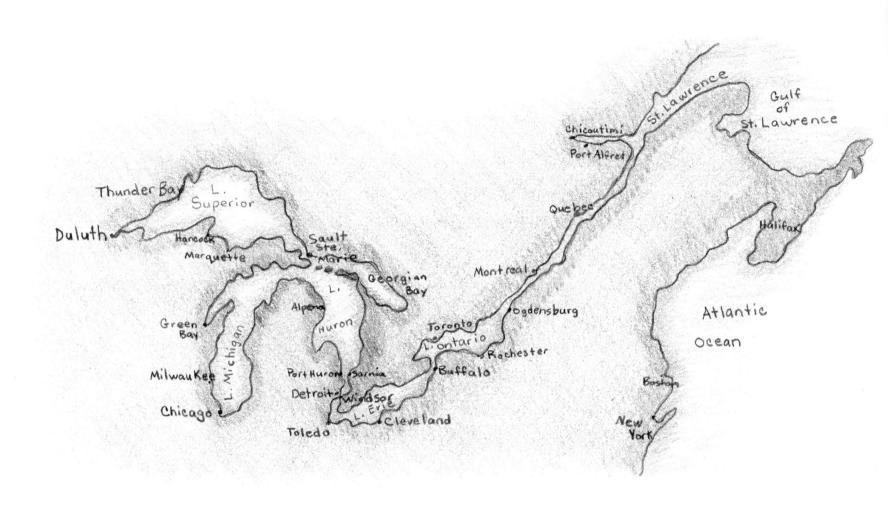

"Mama, where do the big boats go?
Where are they sailing, do you know?"

They go as far as the north winds blow,

with tons of cargo down below.

Day and night, in all kinds of weather,

they travel alone, or sometimes together,

past the wind-swept sand dune ridges,

even under famous bridges.

They see sunrises and sunsets

and fishermen setting out their nets.

The captain and his ready crew
have many jobs that they must do:

hatches to check, potatoes to boil,

yards of dock line to make a big coil,

loading up on iron ore,
until there isn't room for more.

Or they carry coal or grain,
unload, and sail away again,

making stops at busy docks,
or changing levels at the locks.

When the cook can't go ashore to buy food from a grocery store,
the groceries will make the trek by boat and crane to freighter's deck.

But sometimes it's the crew who ride
from the ship's deck to dockside!

The sturdy tug and pilot boats
help to keep the ships afloat.

Coast Guard boats are ready, too,
to make sure all is safe for you.

The ships pass many happy faces

and even join in sailboat races!

Then they sail into the night
by glowing moon and bright spotlight.

"Tell me Mama, how do you know
all the places the big ships go?"

I once sailed the lakes, and so
that's how I know where the freighters go.

Marlene Miller is an artist, writer, and poet, as well as a preschool teacher. She has been writing and illustrating stories and poems since childhood. A native of Port Huron, Michigan, she spent many summer evenings on the shores of Lake Huron with her parents, watching freighters spotlight fishing boats. Her illustrations capture the wonder that freighters gave her as a child. Marlene's other interests are camping and hiking, kayaking and sailing, climbing trees, enjoying nature, and, of course, reading to and playing with her triplet grandsons and two granddaughters.